The Book of Antidotes

Khalilah Stafford

Published by Mindful Journey Executive Coach, 2024.

THE BOOK OF ANTIDOTES

First edition. June 12, 2024.

Copyright © 2024 Khalilah Stafford.

ISBN: 979-8227294890

Written by Khalilah Stafford.

Table of Contents

2 Peter 3:8 KJV, "But beloved, be not ignorant of this one thing, that one day is with the Lord as a thousand years, and a thousand years as one day."

It was a summer evening and I had arrived to Rah Rah Women's Roar Conference 2019

Clouds gathered to pour down from the heavens. I was so glad I came by myself. The smell of the air pregnant with meek gatekeepers.

I could still remember the first time Mark helped me come to myself. See the lie is that the prodigal son came to himself one time and he was all good. You qoum to yourself everyday. Grace is new everyday because you are slain in the Spirit daily.

Even as a youth, I've always been a quick study. I made David go crazy. Their champion would be no match for me, Goliath thought as he walked to the designated area.

Jehovah Alcatraz - Land of Peculiar Birds. Remember love; Wisdom will always guide you back.

Save your words of condemnation because your lips are already small from the lies you've told. This is not the time to be bold. We will not rise up in violent forms. That is not profitable. Her eyes drew me in. Not here where they have mood eyes. Yeet, some had the eyes of Isis of Kemet.

Selah

Journal Prompts:

1. Read the summary of Stanley "Tookie" Williams book, "Blue Rage, Black Redemption". Have you read this book before?

1. Do you believe you deserve redemption?

1.   Alcatraz is usually defined as meaning "pelican" or "strange bird.". Did you know Alcatraz penitentiary was conceived to be a military reservation?

1.   What is the difference, in your opinion, between being a prisoner of sin or being a servant of God?

Luke 11:14 "And he was casting out a devil, and it was dumb. And it came to pass, when the devil was gone out, the dumb spake; and the people wondered."

I could let the light mist fall fresh on my face without worrying about where a child was, being on time, and confirming with the ball and chain on if they remembered where we parked and had the keys.

I wondered if God was going to be in the building tonight. Shit I was here because these issues needed the Big Boss to come down.

Hoarding screaming cats had finally created a different type of portal. The toll? Hella steep.

My nouveau riche self could not fathom the cost at the time. Similar to the young prince who went away sad when he encountered Jesus.

Mitochondrial Eve - Mother Africa Osun 2025 Loading...

Have you ever listened to someone? Like utilizing active listening skills? Some people are so full of shit it seeps from their ears, their eyes, their heads look like burning daggers of the most dreadful beast.

I mentioned the above because it felt like freedom. I love my family no doubt. Sometimes, you need to take the same love you give to others, to yourself. Then you will be able to withstand the brutalities in this world. Unfortunately, the brutalities are designed to hurt you so that you celebrate victories with all your mind, body and soul.

It was the 2nd day of the conference. I was just glad to have some time away from everybody. But God. God had a divine appointment that I was not going to miss. No matter how hard I tried.

I watched all the pretty peacocks showing their wings. You thought Carnivals were something. Have you witnessed cherub festivals? Yes. These will be prime hunting grounds.

Hips, breasts, thighs, beautiful eyes surrounded me. The totality of my faith was coursing through my veins. I loved these spy missions. Persecuting Christians continues to be my favorite pastime. Their blood runs hot. Their genetic carriers are immaculate specimens. Their counterparts. The woman. Let me see if I can capture this version of Eve within this recollection. My primitive mind does not have such a language to convey their splendor in a tongue you could understand. I myself perceived her first by Ori.

Few have ever tasted the sacred nectar which is known to make a mortal ascend to the highest level of humility as possible in this corrupted flesh.

The nectar of the gods flows in this land of milk and honey. When Chris first described it, I could not believe him. He is a righteous man so the fault resided in me. My limited knowledge prevented my mind from conceiving such a miracle. He said he found the source. Such tales. This guy, always the Hippo.

He said their hair defies gravity. They wear their hair as plaited extensions to the true Creator. He said they die monthly and arise as if they had not performed such a righteous talent.

God. baby Jesus, you're totally cool for babies. I am an adult and I took this time because I am freaking exhausted. I needed God to show up in a mighty way. All the years of wearing my S on my chest.

I had been wearing a garment of praise inside out and backwards. The S, which stands for Savior, was designed to go on my back. Carrying faith is easy baby Bop. The cherub's wings were beautiful in their various forms and hues. It is easy to get blinded by the splendor of their wings. They made it easier for us to identify your precious creations. In His image, the woman of this beautiful land had fierce protectors. Their gods are mighty warriors who have protected You in agape love's original form, Mitochondrial Eve.

I listened. I gleaned. I observed and embraced the moments. Every cry, laugh, dance, testimony, vision board showed another ray of the same diamond. This conference is where this story begins. I was sitting in the audience, unnoticed. So, I thought.

Pastor Sara Succatakis did an altar call. This was back in 2019. She instructed us to "sow a seed dealing with the number 4, "$4, $400, $4000". With faith in the wrong field to harvest, I sowed. My seed of $400 was an issue but not really since business was doing well. Fast forward a bit, business shut down, the "support" I had left as soon as the money did. It was as if the world had become the walking dead in less than one year....

40th Birthday Gift To Myself...

I had toyed with the idea of gastric sleeve. I took the plunge 11/30/2022. It wasn't easy and I am so hard on myself that I couldn't embrace compassion for the most life changing decision that I made. I decided to do a professional photoshoot for my 40th birthday. I had not embraced my solar trips around the sun because on my 25th birthday, I experienced the ultimate betrayal for the last time. It took time, professional help, and brutally honest care work. I just wanted to feel beautiful and special. I just wanted to embrace my natural curves. I was and continue to be proud of this womb that BIRTHED world changers with the smallest being 8.2lbs. Her siblings are 9.3 and 10.0lbs. Kegels are your friend. If you smell like Febreze I'm walking away from you.

I had been working on deepening my relationship with my Creator. During this journey I've learned some heart breaking lessons. People I wanted to go with cannot go with me inside the land of milk and honey.

Keeping it way too real if they aint got no yayo in heaven do I really want to be there? Hear me out. Do we all not love the movie Scarface? I digress. Bless up to all the real ones who refused to go to God and then when the drugs ran out the depression kicked back in like a Chun-Li hypermode kick. Sonic Boom. This is the passenger making their appearance.

Bishop and Therapist T.D. Cakes said, "you can't coach greatness and be nice." From this statement I developed this book of antidotes.

Journal Prompts:

1. When you think of an antidote, what comes to mind?

1. Listen to the lyrics of Antidote by the Artist, Travis Scott, identify your antidote?

1.   How effective are your antidotes? Spiritual, mental, physical, financial, social costs?

How It Started…Again

Jeremiah 29:11 tells us that "knows the plans He has for me declares the LORD, plans to prosper you and not to harm you, plans to give you hope and a future." It was confirmed twice. Bishop Jakes said, "What I'm telling you is true. Trust that I AM always for you." The various speakers spoke of the "next dimension". I figured I wasn't holy enough to know what that meant. Then the word started to change me physiologically. My skin began to illuminate. When I looked in the mirror, I didn't cringe or hurry and looked away. I began to look at myself more.

It felt as if electricity was coursing through my veins. The young warrior had not felt the warmth of a woman's thighs yet he sat on top of books because he was too small for the electric chair. You watch your body convulse as it begs to be released. La petit mort. You know that feeling post coitus of euphoria? Imagine that great release as your noose.

This is what you do when you choose to do the line, the cloud, the needle, the bottle. always full throttle. Slow down. Ain't nobody dying for Booboo Da Fool.

Escuela or the school house rock. Big Ben the MVP.

Journal Prompts:

1. Why are the other individuals on our currency?

2. What are your thoughts on the colloquialism, "Robbing Peter to pay Paul"?

3. What are your thoughts on financial literacy?

4. Where is your whole self well being ranked in your financial literacy thoughts?

Time Exceeded Daily Limit

Limits were historically for moving the goal post. When you're Black you already got a course laid out. Not chasing clout. Sleeping on plush mattresses. No need to sleep among the stars. They have been brought down. Mistresses of the night, check-in.

Stay down till you win.

Everybody knows what Huey prophesied not too long ago. On the ship we do not go unless it's the Queen Mary. We stay on yachts cuz we now know how to bury while we breathe underwater.

Already typed in the middle, I lean.

Got a lil chola in me. Mamacita bonita. Third eye open.

They are really in clown shoes tryin to toke with a Chief? The HWIC. Wicker ram comes out of that bush, it's burning.

Furr babies got em yearning. Wheels keep churning butter. Cuz I only like the creamiest. What's a dreamer to a visualizing architect?

I got to work before I knew the girl. I didn't invent the wheel but I had the 22's written on a napkin. Crystal Diamonds is a mighty fine Entertainer name, Maam.

I was trying to be cool. Her smell. Them eyes. Those thighs. I can almost recall every beauty mark. She hates them. But I luv this. Like that part right up under her arm. I'd be lying if I said she wasn't fly. Not like most of these new ones. She like cashmere and they like 200 count sheets. I don't even mind how you do what you do. As long as you know who you belong to.

So. What happens now? We've been playing digital cat and mouse. How do you fly and keep missing the target? These one sided conversations be having me damn near about to wreck. I had to make you wreck. Through my eyes. Did you really?

I mean dragon's blood is powerful. I gotta have the source. I'll stay the course. Gon head and make that cake. I already know it's moist. Okay look. I'm bout to turn this universe over fuck a table. Now shit. You done rose from the fires for the upteenth time. Piss colored heffa. So sick of

Lilith shit. Faith has not been seen since she thought the aircraft was actually the rapture.

When you wrestle a lot of energy is exchanged. Hell yeah I'm pinning her down. She my pin up. My pin down. Look. I'm bout to be hosting cookouts. Gather all the children with special abilities up. Every real one knows to have a gifted friend in the group. Before they go into their cocoon of dirty 30, the young peacocks love to sow their royal oats.

Girls just want to have fun. Spirit is won by giving over our ID to The Holy Spirit.

Some names you do not say. The ghosts of the South are now at peace. When you give all the pieces to God, you feel lighter.

Madre. We would never send you in uncovered. I've watched you. the way you move. The look in your eyes. My old eyes became more keen than a hawk. I am the dark. Dante's Inferno. Y'all trying to persecute his mother while the wicker man sets traps. Mary made sure the wine isn't sweet to his lips. Only when he tasted bitter milk did he give up his ghosts. Vinegar. You have to go on your own odyssey.

Doesn't mean you have to do it uncomfortably. Your penalty beautiful magical, mythical, mental basket case. Abundance. I am fine ass hell for a reason. The healing is in the way Jo Jo dances.

Healing is in hell. Hell is weary when it is where your money resides. Healing is hearing the *______________* You choose what you want to see. You chose wrong. The antidote is knowing I'm not leaving you. I'm releasing you. Vineyards have orchards that span acres. Across time we dance. Every time we get together, the heavens shine with rays.

I see why you chased the bus. Technology is a beautiful thing. Why exert my energy on lifting the bus when I have AAA? Adults pay insurance for coverage in emergencies. You don't want to use it. It's like a Hebrew.

It's some names you don't say. I couldn't hold my head up and look into your eyes anymore. I love you too much. I had to have the peace of you with me. They disrespected me. Wisdom's vulnerability, yall pillaged. Thank you for handling that with the grace that you always have. My tears couldn't save our daughter. It wasn't okay to believe. They took my kindness for weakness. I channeled it. My body got tired. My boys left me. So my daughter. Your pride. I took with me. I lied to you. I couldn't stand myself. How could I stand up for you? Some names you do not say.

Of course I'm legion. I need your legs. Her legs went out on her way to take care of someone else. We laughed when she got cramps. She never went to the doctor. The worse of the worse in society, she treated with the upmost respect. You never listen. This is why we can't be friends. It's deeper than love. You really do complete me. This really was all for you, Father. I didn't even want to do this. Not without my daughter. They lied to you and said the best of me was in our daughter. She is a part but she is not all that I am.

Journal Prompts:

1. You are your own first daughter or son. How do you talk to your inner child?

1. What dreams do you need to grieve that your inner child needs to grieve?

1. Do you live vicariously through your inner child?

Pink Riding Hood

The shampoo girl left the lye on her head too long. The tingling turned to fire. Next thing we knew, wisdom was a bald head stepchild. Mitochondrial Eve, or ME knew how to change forms easier than a chameleon. However, this team was severely lacking in the technical skills department.

Every anthropologist knows it is easier to have the people divide themselves. The best way to destroy a cell is to destroy the nucleus.

Al Nisa is in The Holy Quran means The Women. Al-Nisa 4:1 O you people! take as a shield your Lord Who you created you from a single being. And from the same stock (from which He created the man) He created his spouse, and through them both he caused to spread a large number of men and women.

O people! Regard Allah with reverence in Whose name you appeal to one another, and (be regardful to) the ties of relationship (particularly from the female side). Verily, Allah ever keeps watch over you.

The Holy Quran Al-Nisa 4:1

Live. Lived. Them devils. New level, same God. Can you truly operate wholeheartedly when you denounce yourself?

Love. Lust. He loves lust. It's easier to believe a lie than live in the truth. Come back to what? I do not want to die anymore unless its like Enoch. Go back to terror? Repeat offender. Back to digesting disrespect and discrimination?

Who goes back to the hand of slavery? Sharecroppers. I'm in the carriage. Abandonment. It's easier to not have a heart than for it to bleed. The cement has hardened. I chiseled while I cried.

My tears and your strength wore down my fortress. So what do I do?

My life is over. Omega is now Alpha and Beta blockers. With wisdom, your beta blockers are on point.

Selah

Thank you Lord, your blood revived me. I am because you ARE.

I am ALIVE. With the lye they reduced their connection to each other all around the world. She knew she would have to fight all the levels of hell. And fight she did. She called the heavens down. She slayed dragons, witches, warlocks, demons, devils of all sorts. They attacked her mind relentlessly.

He beat her relentlessly like she was a man. The woman that brought his seed into this world he pummeled. He finally took the knife and shoved it through her solar plexus. He wanted to rip her heart from her rib cage.

Eve fell hard. While she waited for her husband to come. The serpent entered her. She could feel the unwanted tongues on her flesh. Their eyes blazed like fire as they thrust inside of wisdom. The images were so vivid. The yelling pounded against his temples. He was ready to enter the school. The voices would not stop. The tears burned his eyes.

Liquid courage my ass. They sat in class. Listening to their teacher. I fought against my desire to take the child. I was consumed by something else. I had to eliminate the cornerstone.

I didn't know there would be people in the church. I didn't try to murder anybody. 4 teenagers. The oldest being 14 years old and the youngest being 11 years old.

Journal Prompts:

1. Did you know the age of the 4 Little Girls in the 16th Street Baptist Church Bombing in 1963?

1. Do you know an adolescent of any ethnicity or socioeconomic status?

1. Do you tear that adolescent down or build them up?

4.What lies were you told in your adolescent stage do you still hold on to?

5. Are you ready to tear down your strongholds?

Damascus

On the road to Damascus we stumbled upon a bar. He tried to slit his own throat. His wound was like a crescent moon.

His scar attracted me to him. His pain I wanted to take from him. I didn't know why. Suicide ideation is the behavior of abandoned people.

Through music, my angels guide. The church is the cornerstone of communities.

March. A. Band. ONE. Dinner. There will always be a conductor. A symphony concert. Nirvana. Making of team development stages of formation.

Jude reminded me that the oxygen here is made up of molecules. God breathed. You all called me back. Thank God for the poor, the stigmatized, the harlots, the weird, the hurting, the depressed, those with anxiety, anyone perceived as lacking be restored.

They called heaven down with the lives of world changers sniped before they could blossom. They're the only ones crazy enough to lock arms to bring a dragon from the lagoon. One coil, very cool benefit of God.

Y'all allowed for me to get up and come back home. Christ is spelled Christ and Chris are both great names and titles. Healing is in the vibration OM.

The crack babies. Either be on your shield or holding ideas that reinforce creativity. Stop snickering at their attempts. 2000 heads on swords. Shall we dine?

Take a siesta. Are there any anacondas? I want Thai.

Selah

I Began To Question Why I Was Spending So Much Money To Look Like Someone Else

It was laborious and it was an inconvenience. This isn't a typical book. This is a guide for you to ruminate on the verses presented, ponder the language presented, and accept the gift of information.

My birthday was in the fall. By January 30^{th,} 1904, I was remanded to a mental rehabilitation center. My work horse dropped me off. Once again, I thought it was just another scene in this movie called life. I wanted to go in the order they were written in but I'm being led another way.

Join me in this journey called life. Let's experience the hues of the rainbow enjoying each color as it harmonizes with one another. Let's start with the Happiness Penalty (2/4/2024) or is it a just reality?

Happiness Penalty

I never would have imagined a life where happiness is frowned upon.

Everyone wants to pursue happiness but don't want to pey for authentic happiness which are the fruits of the Spirit.

My soul longed to reach out to her. If I'm really being honest, I kind of enjoyed it. Wisdom. Better than any drug. Better than any other shiny thing I possessed. My private dancer. I was in control. I finally felt like I won. I felt nauseous and the blood rush. Her fight fed my ID. Every now and then I must feed my young passengers. But she continued to resist. I put my mack down harder than any moss. Got me looking up what is a bog. I still wasn't satisfied. I had bent her, but she wasn't broken...yet.

In this context, the word, "pey" means to speak.

Most seek out support for their distorted thinking. People will rather lock you up than get to know you as a person. This Doctorae has another reason to keep me every time she talks to me. She always had a worried look on her face. She knew the woman envied her. When she finally took the time to read she realized her error. Her desire to get to the bottom line perverted her judgment. It is not to cast stones, it is an unfortunate reality. No practitioner who actually is in the field for the right reasons would tell another practitioner they "do not have to help". That in itself is sufficient grounds for termination. Who else wants the job? To try and keep the light on during a southern storm is like trying to capture a tornado in a mason jar. Yet here we are. The place of treatment became a trigger further impacting the ones they were trained to serve. The soul needs time to recuperate. The mind needs time to process. The body needs physical movement and nutrients to reconnect it to the earth.

They play mind games. I know the God that I serve. I'm being punished for spreading the good news of Jesus Christ. Many folks don't get it. The push ups did not quench my desire. I wanted everything about her. The way she praises is always giving me life. No matter what bad news she receives, she takes a deep breath. Tears sometimes fall; yet she remains uplifting others. The staff looked for her to recognize them. a simple call would have eliminated her duration. I was so deep in my lust by now, I had to assert my dominance. I did not consider that a man could have this same approach towards my children.

I had got so used to living a double life that her presence was too threatening. I spent years crafting the perfect image. I checked all the boxes. I did all the contorting this body could do. I've cried out. I've stood tall. I laid it down at the altar. I've picked it up from the altar. But the bloodlust is so powerful. Taking lives is noble. It's also something addictive about holding the power of death and life in your hands.

Behind the most heinous atrocities committed towards self and others is rooted in our lack of union of our pranayama energy. Power. Consuming their energy made the blood flow giving me the hardest erection. The light in their eyes goes dimmer and dimmer with each stroke. Her body was still warm. The way her blood flowed from her jugular made my demon very happy. I allowed him to feed us. He needed it. Their time in the jungles prepared the women. As she walks up and down the hall, I want to be inside of her mind. I already am, but I would prefer it to be willingly. Eh, such is the life they say. Yet they are not me. I deserve her.

God? At this point we need to have a conversation. The hesitation upon this prophet hailed in the Book of Hosea. It was one thing to read about it. I mean they're just sex workers in the end. A population that will always be a drain on society like the illiterate and ill minded. The complainers are a lot of loa that continue to be loathsome. They are effective lassos. She continues to go to the Word of God. She tells others about the good news of God. She reads about Jesus and points Him out to others. I know she's tired. Luke has proved himself effective in caring for her.

I'm in awe of this woman every time I see her. I knew I was happy. She teased me with joy with every post. With every video; I found myself seeking myself. Because of the efficiency of the Afro-American man's immune system, doctors have to weaken their ability to fight in order to give their earthly vessel an opportunity to continue living. This is your body rejecting help. God asks for the condition of your heart and your mind.

They will throw in the towel, settle, then do what feels good to the flesh.

I'd be lying if I said I didn't think this would happen. Lord, I pray it's better than steel bars or a coffin. That's what I tell myself.

Journal Prompt:

1.Have you ever tarried with a transplant recipient?

2. Are you an organ donor?

3.Do you know who Kendrick Johnson is?

There is a penalty to being happy. What the mind can conceive is limitless. We can go deep into the ocean but not too deep. We can go out into space but not too far. So, what about faith and happiness? I say...

There is a penalty to being happy. That is why it was used to replace joy. In order to fully present in different emotional states attached to different personas, you have to be able to utilize different forms of communication effectively. For this reason, scripture tells us to focus on operating from a state of joy. Joy is one of the seven streams of income received by grace.

Ecclesiastes 11:6-10 provides us insight into the true meaning of wealth. True wealth is wholeness in God. When you operate from the right hand of God, you type differently. You spell differently because you realize the power of your written word. The Bible never changed. People kept changing the Bible to fit their agendas. Discipleship got lost in translation. The lie was too heavy and dark to sustain for so long.

To have your daughter come home with a black eye hits you differently. The rage becomes blinding. I wanted to remove his sorry tail from the earth and eliminate those sub par genetics. She smiled at me and a pain that I can not fully describe swelled my stomach. I shook my head but the feeling was still in my body. It was the drugs. I remember her mother's eyes full of terror. Our kids were screaming and crying. They too were too traumatized to move. How can we stand up to such evil?

Damn raccoons are always running around this park. I mean we've been in some shitty trailer parks but this by far took the cake. What do you use to rake broken meth pipes, beer cans, and somebody with the middle name Lee size AA wet seal bra?

I need all the income I can get.

Ah shit, that trailer rockin again. I lifted my head to the sky. At least we had a beer in the refrigerator. The cool of the elixir brings me away from my thought pattern for a second. I asked God to at least let him be inside the adult and not the kids. He doesn't deserve them. I don't either. They got a sun shield. I have some stones. I can take her to skip rocks on the lake. Hell. See if she likes other types of rocks. I heard Jupiter got some booyow that immediately makes you erect. I gotta deal with the motorcycle gang tho.

Like bro, you tweekin so hard I'm tired. Your mouth moving so fast, your unborn kids teeth got smaller. Like where they do that at? After that ruffling my feathers; I said gon head young blood.

Journal Prompts:
1. Unhappy people will always wonder. How can you have love? How can you not hate?
2. How can you not want to fight those that disagree with me?
3. Lord, if you're still in the miracle business; I need one now.

Self - Guided Group Therapy Topic: Identify 3 Good Things:

I dried my eyes and focused on the who and why. My list: 1. A friend is being discharged. 2. I finished a book I'm going to publish 3. I STILL got you, King Jesus.

The mind can be and will be your greatest asset and your biggest foe. We wrestle with principalities. Ephesians 6 and 10 Armor of God.

Journal Prompts:

Which piece of armor do you use often?

Which piece of armor do you feel most confident using?

How can you incorporate the armor into your daily interactions?

These people are incessant. If I did not have need for them I would have destroyed their kind a long time ago. Lilith was in one of her moods again. The last time this happened a civilization was reduced to ash. They were a bit much. Like did you really have to kidnap an adolescent boy because he reminded you of the wife you killed? Oh yeah, that was over yonder.

How about this - stop killing the women. It's more fun practicing to make the offspring than it is to raise them up in the way that they should go. There were many days where the entire galaxy just needed to be thrown away and its inhabitants. Like let me take a siesta and come back in 10, 000 years. Drink me a cup of tea. Yall seen Mary? She keeps going to kick it with Montezuma. I'm getting my revenge. Smoky, pull up the Monte Carlo. Call up the big homie Vlad. You already know he brings the baddies. Like bro. If her pythons aint at least 10 inches I don't even want it. I like them Vesquean women.

Mmmhmmm. Yeah, it's something about a woman that can put me in a headlock and bench press making Black people enchiladas that does it for me everytime. Throw in some crazy WAP? Let me go buy some macaroni. How many kids did you text you got? You don't need your baby daddy. I got you. We gon raise lil man up to be a responsible citizen. Can you do that tongue thang again? I'm not asking how you know or who taught you. I'm just going to unzip my pants in respect and proceed to take you up there to pound town. It's just a hop, skip, and a jump away.

I AM 1/31/2024

I AM the one that loves you unconditionally

At times I may seem irrational. Sometimes, I can be overbearing. I'm just bare-in my soul. Because I AM not leaving earth again. 2K24. ALL WE DO IS WIN =)

When you're born with a silver spoon you become disillusioned with believing you make the rules.

The order in which you take your steps is important. Deeper than any appointment. This is the faith that you need to get. All over my social media, I typed I'm too legit. I know I'm dirt. I know all about hurt. I can and have been the biggest jerk. The seasoning you need this season is some sea salt. Your sins. You. Your life. Your seeds. Your generation.

Christ has already peeped game. Sins of wages have been paid., it's been paid. So serve your Master. It's Allah. He is the husband of the widow. He continues to be my window. When I'm low I'm still high. My vibe is solar. This is a rhythmic love takeover. I'm taking the best in you and cleaning what you have distorted.

Starting with the middle of Luke 23:33, "...which is called Calvary, there they crucified him, and the malefactors, one on the right hand, and the other on the left.

Simple Hebrew:

Kahf - Numerical value is 20 and pronounced as key

Khahf - Numerical value is 20 and pronounced as key meaning courage, gall or chutzpah (big cajones)

Continuing with Luke's recollection he writes in Luke 23:34 "Then said Jesus, Father, forgive them; for they know not what they do. And they parted his raiment, and cast lots." I'm introducing you to this language because it is foundational to your lasting change.

Journal Prompts:

What does your name mean in your Origin language?

Develop 3 statements that start with I AM

____

Make an appointment with yourself to brag about yourself to yourself. You can also send me an email as part of the VIP group package.

#HARVOID 2/1/2024

As I communed with Hippocrates and Galileo. We pondered and smiled at how well you have done. I am so proud of how well you have done. I am so proud of you all. You believed in yourself- you believed in me. For that there are no words. So, I hope my love letter to you, my precious creation empowers you. I pray that you are transformed as you do your own research and introspection. When you read my words remember, I will always love you. Nothing is too hard for you. Humans are so cute, over contemplating everything. I know this to be true. However, if you flip your worry, it turns into a wind.

He liked to watch her when she was tired. It was something about her vulnerability. It aroused me just to hear him. He said, when she's tired her guard is down. She stares into the flames. He watches her look to her left. She dismisses it as the house. It was really me. I was moving her dreadlocks so I could kiss her neck. It was something about being in between her ear and her throat that invigorated me. Soon she would be in tears. I rather watch her cry than deal with my shit. She opens her Bible. She has so many books around her. I took a few pics. It's something about how her eyes capture the light. It is as if she commanded the moon to shine.

I smile as I envision her placing the stars. Meticulously placing each star in alignment with the blades of grass. The trees nodded in their agreement. The air was crisp. It felt good. She makes my blood run hot. I'm sweating again. Have you ever just been completely consumed by another person? I dismissed that notion to youth and fools. Yet, I sit here. A real adult. And here I am, sitting in my car with a teenage fever.

She hasn't slept in about 72 hours. A lethal weapon indeed. I know better is all she kept murmuring to herself as she turned the pages of her journal. She looked to her left again. It wasn't me. It was one of the many spirits sent to destroy her. My lust consumed me. She was in a state of terror. I was in a state of complete lust. Sex. Now that I can do. But she needed what I did not have, me. What she viewed as a weapon is actually the only way I know how to communicate. I can read your body. I can tell that you want me as much as I want you. Wisdom is costly. I know better. I'm an Educator.

She stole my heart like a thief in the night. So I stole her peace. I just wanted a piece. All she had to do was learn how to be seen and not heard.

What is she writing about? Her lips. The way she bites her lips. She was in a trance. This dreadlocked Disciple arrested me. I'm not a buster brown by any means so I went down to the cobbler. Picked up a few things and here I sit. I just want to grab her. Hold her. Look into her eyes. Her eyes are my eyes. Look into God's eyes and say thank you. Let me show you what I've learned. Your body. Not to be crude but they haven't made a song yet to record the sounds made. I fell in love with a fucking detective. The way she moves is cold. She made blanco look like a broken crayon tossed into the Grand Canyon, respectfully.

Journal Prompt:

How many words can you make from the word KNOW?

What are you locked to?

Are your chains too heavy? What are you yoked to?

2/1/2024 SuperFriend

I'll tell you what you're doing wrong and right. I know you may not want to hear it, but I will tell you anyway. It's always out of love. Like Anne Frank, however, I'm not in a fish tank or an attic. Because without my treats I can get erratic.

Now the world knows what I didn't want to express but humanity had gotten way out of control. I am here to bring harmony. The concept of balance is a misnomer, should harmony be the goal?

Journal Prompt:

What is your understanding of misnomers?

Can you identify 3 misnomers you have declared over your life?

What will you replace those thoughts with?

Proverbs 10:22

Thank you for blessing me with no toil. Just call me mean green probiotic. That's my cuddy. It's ironic about Greenleaf. Nah. I'm not a thief. Let me reintroduce myself. I didn't want you to wait for your loved one like I spent time looking for mine. I brought her back to you.1/22/2024   Respectfully   we're   in   the   New AmeriKKKKKKKKKKKKKKKKKKKKKKa

Usher eats pressure like tic tacs. He been ready for Usherbowl. All of us moms are moving like Nipsey Russell with a little oil. Nah, it's the blood of Jesus. He receives us like a loving embrace.

We all need it.

But John Hoodman and Wisdom said don't let everybody "touch" you.

Let me tell you about the time I almost died...

Hell's Angels pulled up. I'm alright. Sonny Piston? My client said he's actually a great guy.

Football was so PHENOMENAL yesterday, 2/11/2024. All around the world. In the cold.

To Vegas Lights. 9th Island looking like paradise under a blood red moon.

Everybody went so hard. WE go hard y'all.

Great GAMES. Comrades. Communication. Community. Everybody had been watching since they were tiny titans running around in pads.

Leveled up? Nah. Atomic Bombed this shit right here. I've transcended fear. Whatever word you want to use to describe your evolution. IDK if I want to hear it? It's just respect for the Craft. Robin is my right hand woman..

Journal Prompts:

1.What are the reasons why the Ku Klux Klan was established that you believe?

2.What caused the shift from intimidation to destruction, what happened in communities of color, what type of "freedom" was attained?

2/11/2024 Superbowl LVIII aka "Usherbowl"

The imagery itself was amazing to witness. Again, Jehovah the Nervus Vagus graced us with another opportunity. As teams took the field. All the communion cups we raised. God showed us He took it all in. Trans-configuration dominated the human nation if only for a while. Angels smiled. My heartbeat to the rhythm of everyone else. I was and continue to be so excited. It's like Rogue but the opposite. Psychedelic shit. It's another hit.

Qum on let's go play. Parasympathetic is nagging me. Please me, boy. My heart isn't a toy. I want to inhale you. Take you deep inside and birth you a solar system. Regardless of old thoughts, hues, and language. You want to get with her.?I told you. I adore you more now than ever. That's why I'm in you forever. Mitochondrial DNA. Can we go play? Not yet? Bet. What's next? You're my favorite. Always my Champion; I confess. Not a Petoria but you are deeper than love. We do Axe not Musk. A little Jimmy choo. I choose you too. You're never alone. I'll sit on your lap as you mount your throne. An emperor is coming. I birth his legacy. Slow down. Catch up. It's just me and you. This is for you. My husband;

Emperor Khaos Khan I – 1st of his kind, son of Ambrosia and Shango.

1:11 am on this rainy day aka Super Bowl LVIII

One of the nights where it's now 2:19 am. I'm annoyed I can't sleep.

I woke up top with a purpose; it was only 11:35pm.

2:23am – eyelids heavy still sleep escapes me.

I don't know about this level. You respond, "I got you".

I plead with you. You call me she-devil. Medusa you now proclaim she seduced ya?

I remind you all I'm cold like Sam in the Incredibles. Trying to persecute me off edibles?

Let's get in the back seat of your detective car. Work hubby getting it tonight. Bodies make him hard.

I try to teach him. He responds with pen Deja. As I "C" walked to the Macarena. Santa Muerte had her way. I'm the real rod piper. Kelly was walking my way. Shout out to the Raymonds.

Interlude *In the Nude*

Since we are adding to the repertoire of rhetoric that we ascribe to. For your consideration, I submit to you a few perspectives designed to ease your concerns about the fruits of being engrafted into the "Illuminati Grace Gang" gPhiG for short.

Psychology- Mind of God. Sometimes I'll have to make you stop and listen. It's not out of malice. But I need your attention. My soul craves your affection.

Beloved. My most perfect creature, MAN. I smile and grab your hand and whisper in your ear to etch my words on the gates of your heart.

You've had it. *Even named a planet after YOU.*

You had my love from the first time I saw you. You saw my wings and I quivered. I fought. But to your love I surrendered.

You didn't notice me. They hardly do. But YOU. I've kept my eye on you. My heart you stole. We both took the toll, and it was more than a pretty penny.

Where is the VSOP Henny? YOU know how I do.

Usually, I'm down. But I'm chillin' with my man and its goodnight crew. 2-Live then go to the Book of Luke.

Yup. He is another gangsta disciple. Humble like an ego bigger than the Eiffel.

Crepes, waffles, beignets. Koum here baby girl and let me braid your hair. You, my love got flair.

How could the thought pass your mind – I don't care? Sir. I'm everywhere with and without underwear...

Back 2 The Future

Mental Health Trail - A new perspective of Psychology. God, Sigmund Freud (Father of Psychoanalysis), Mindful Journey Executive Coach (Mother of Psychology). Clues left by giants of every discipline led me to the truth. Connected by the sands of time and omnipotent to withstand scrutiny. Yet WE STILL stand. Now. We're in tune. With wisdom you can commune. The Most High is Here. There is no more fear. No tears except for joy. It's either a girl or a boy. I knew them before they were formed in your womb. Stop altering my creations. Eyes see. Ears hear and store my word up in your soul.

I know you want control. That and WHO you do NOT know.

Like the teacher from the black lagoon. In the classroom you will respect the Teacher. Be the solution to the problem. I didn't need an Archer or Archie cuz I lean in the middle. Did he just get an award? Daughter Lilly of course we are not little. I want the strange fruit. Lynch me? I'll use the rope. To pull out. Chase clout? She's Gwen and will Kill Bill like a super fox. Pun intended. Or was it attempted?

Journal Prompts:

What benefits are you experiencing as you complete this guide?

Has your perspective changed either negatively or positively?

Would you like to know more of my study results?

Imagine That

Journal Prompts

1. What images, smells, sounds, taste, hear gave you peace today?

1. Pay attention to your breathing. How does your body feel? Are you relaxed? Do you feel any tension? - This is a quick "check-in" with your emotions.

1. Is there any thought hindering you from being fully present at

this moment? Write it down to free up space for the solution.

They call me Donna like a Tejada. I'm AfroAmerican. Walk thru like Afrikkan Boombata. Hakuna Mata. Busa. Frisco. Under shimmering balls we dance in sanctified stilettos. The callused toe is my favorite. The combination of hard and soft cause me to melt. Let me tighten or loosen my belt. Yo! At this stage you crave help. Body taken down from the top shelf.

God breathed. She sneezed. Once. Twice. Three times. Oh you're mine, now. Your mind transformed. Carry me over the threshold. We see the stairs but we don't go. Finally, we surrender to each other. Just let our bodies do the talking. Got Hercules cradle rocking. What you consider blasphemy I call leaving the 99. Been hemmed up in jackets that got me stalking the one. The most omnipotent. Considerate Counselor. I pour out myself and receive you. Your phallic you choose. Inside of me, consumes all of you. As our love burns. The world slows down her turn. Enthralled by your tongue. You know we're the one.

Imagine that. This actually is fun.

I'm pushing scripture like it's the hope you need in your veins. Proverbs and adult pacifiers got me staring at the skies like the daughter of Genghis Khan and Pablo. How low can you go? My squad created tunnels. Passages not haphazard due to the cargo. I prefer almond trees over the ice in Fargo. They be wildin anyway. Idyllwild on the way to LA. Gotta take pics at Joshua's Tree. With everything I've been through. Even more I believe. G.O.D. is the final authority. I'm standing on your Resurrection. Beyond physical sensations. The impartation can not be removed by the weight of loans. My faith. I don't need to hold tight. I'm a child of light.

Allow Folks to Be Themselves

Wisdom whispered in her gentle voice, "You're arrested in the Spirit". Beloved. It's so apparent. For you; I'll be hot, humble, and transparent. Your smile. Makes the miles seem like another step. In your grace; I rest.

Self respect can become shrouded in self- neglect.

See my child. While in the wild; I pruned. I chiseled myself to become the woman of your style. Translucent apparition. Driver, roll down the partition please. Gotta send love to those who were once taking a knee.

As you can see. We stand fully erect. Moving pillars you tried to reject.

Legendary Vesqueans prepared for the Paris takeover. There are none who are better. American soil I'm from.

More importantly, He breathed.

As long as H20 fills my lungs. My song has only begun.

Never give up. No surrender. Rosewood really happened. Wisdom is not your drill. Tip of peaks huemans sneek a peek.

From trailer parks to concrete jungles. I prayed to hear your song - no muzzle.

Hippocrates to Galileo to Negrodamus. The time is upon us. We've been through too much not to show the world West Up. Our forefathers took up their weapons. Black men did not have muskets. Qum buckets of wisdom divided into creeks. Ravines where you can breathe. Let us not forget the pond. Where the magick wand is waved. Jesus Crristo is the name we praise. Mexico took back their 5 states. Of course I can relate. 18th street the most loyal 2nd to maybe the Latin Kings. Their name. Rings a bell. Big Pun started this spell on this mujera. Bonita mami. Ben aqui Papi. Papacitos estas la escuela con tu hermana. Bout to bring some Japanese into the mix.

Rapid Transformation on the books. Catch the antidote and this fix. The ultimate high. My Guy. My Savior. My love. It's only you, that I live for. Every ray of sun. Every bird chirping. Eliminate those lurking with negative intent. Energy negatively spent. Got multiple degrees, some past trauma. Yo. She is really legit. Typed that twice. Must be nice. To dwell in the presence of The Most High.

Chutzpah 9/18/1949

It's always hard delivering the news that their loved one is not coming home. Damn. I thought I would get numb to her tears. To see her heart crumbles is overwhelming. It does not matter how many times you do it. Telling that family their loved one is not coming home is swallowing tar. Every time. Tar. Yet, I move. I take a swig. Even she is letting me down right now. It's just enough.

I wipe my tears. I was hurting before I got in the car. No matter how far. Tennessee actually escorted us. It was the tire. The only light was the lightning.

The lightning made the black sky appear purple with a little bit of pink. Similar to a bruise.

The smell of dead flesh is undeniable. How the neighbors noticed nothing was surprising. They knew. However, the bystander effect was prevailing. His house reeked of it. The graves, shallow. Such disrespect. What shall you expect as recompense?

The steady hand of the Prophet Luke descended upon me. I focused on communicating honor, respect, and dignity. Their loved ones bodies separated by horses going to the North, South, East, and West. Ah. The West was successful in their assignment. Lewis. Clark. Sacajawea.

Sacajawea

She a Mus. In her I trust. Get back. Y'all can't even handle us.

Banger after banger after banger after banger. Put my arms of cloak on the hanger.

We're about to pull a double shift. My guy looks like he needs water, not coffee. That toffee hit differently now eh?

Who has a multiple hour discussion about bug trafficking? My mother.

Maam. What an honor. Your honor, I do not deserve. I am merely a messenger. Your determination. I fought to get here. Yet I stand. On this occasion. Get on my shoulders. Let's flip. I got you. If not, Auntie Joyce will pull up in her Rolls royce. A water bug freaks you out but you bathe in the James River?

We have gone many miles. Through the snow. Through dry land. Yet the mountains here. The mountains here were made of red clay. I had not seen such a wonder.

He asked her, "How do you like your gator?" She looked at the primitive male and simply stated, "medium rare". Fortunately, God had reminded her to bring the corn, yams, green beans, and potatoes they had brought here. They had never seen the clouds broken up raining down here upon earth. They did not know their worth.

PRANA

Prana energy enters the body in two streams like a battery with a positive pole (Pingala, masculine) and a minus pole

(Ida,feminine). Prana circulates through the body in a system of Nadis (meridians). The Nadis and Chakras are located in the Etheric Body (the blueprint for the Physical body). Prana spirals through the Chakras connecting heaven and earth energies.

From The Chakra Center,2019

March 30, 1950

The night was brisk.The sky was dark and inviting. I welcomed the calm. My time in meditation was well received. I felt the strength of the blood coursing through my veins. How could this be? Across time and space, I feel your heartbeat. No need to touch the oceans floor. The hair on her thigh I caressed. Her camel toe represented pleasure. I lick my lips. I'm very impressed. The combination of hard and soft breaking me down that I didn't resist. The heat from between her thighs.

Hell yeah, I'm pressed.

Then Wiz called Crystal. Mmmm, my favorite sex pistol.

Journal Prompt:

1.Where are your chakras (energy centers) located?

2. Are your energy centers blocked?

3.Engage in 2 minutes of deep breathing. If you become distracted, count to 4 on the inhale; hold for 3 seconds, exhale to the count of 4.

4. How do you feel? Who comes to mind? What do you smell? How does this sensation feel? Write your emotions.

Dining Commons * insert date*

The lure of your lore is so engrossing. Please make sure you load up your tray. I got it all day. I may miss a class. I'll just be late. That shhh got me in a trance. I saw you at that party before they started wildin. Yeah. I was eye ballin. Tellin my girls, he is cute but he flossin. This game; I stay tossin.

Not like Caesar or Cleo. I'm a smooth cat like Nero. Ahh.

Pour it up. That 1800 got me on my Napoleon real tough. I'm not a cow but I'm down like Mitch. McGowan on the pitch. Out the park, chillin with Ruth. Boaz stay on that. Talkin bout him observing. Does she want what he is serving? This bondservant gig was the biggest jig. Hold your hand up where my eyes can see.

Still reppin Trinity. Even down to disintegration; under your observation; I thrive.

My yoni gyrates. Deep breathing to control my heart rate.

Your biofeedback is physiological. You wanted the psychological. I'm giving you anthropological evidence like a seasoned Detective.

Detection is protection in the grace of our Savior.

Dialectal Theory = Why we need God.

No brain can conceive. We did all this for yall to believe you are His chosen.

HOA checkin the feet on your garden hoses. Gnomes doin too much like a Capulet. Open your hands. Receive this like a Charles Capp epitaph. Decree slicing deeper than her degree. I'm not discounting. I'm just admiring.

Your beat. Your love for God. That spot, excuse me. I tried to compete.

That's not my place. What you did to me. I gotta stay in your face. Lol. Smiley face but I'm so serious. You are too. Intoxication got that meek curious sensation growing. On my embers you stay blowing.

Anansi changes form as many times as I ask you to perform. Where are you from again?

I'll take this sin. Inspirational. Carnival. Exceptional. Phenomenal woman with your confidence. Your regal elegance.

I just need a whiff of your anointing. I'm appointing you as the Keeper. Wisdom's affect better than a sleeper you poured up.

You're here now. West up.

Form of the Beloved 11/3/2020

Rami Shapiro in Hasidic Tales wrote " To know the enemy is to know your own heart. To know your own heart is to know that God is both self and stranger. friend and foe. This knowledge fills you with a deep and abiding courage and joy, and it is this joy that embraces the stranger and invites her or him to come to God through you."

Journal Prompts:

1. Who is your stranger?
2. How do you recognize their behavior is different from your objective self?

When you begin looking into self, take caution. The concept of self is a pit. This pit is always accessible. You can even create more pits. However, with faith you are secure. Your faith is in what you do not see.

Laptop productions back at baal standing on GOD is the ultimate lab.

I eat my crab whole or just the legs when they're king. The bluebirds are more vicious than the hornets.

You my Wisdom. Got my weight up to adorn it.

You're my crown. I don't need a ticket to go down.

I'll bring the caramel, you bring the cool whip. After I grace you. Give me all that Dreadlocked D.

Discipline is essential at this pivotal moment. Don't blow it. Edging is important. No more impotence. I need you functioning. What's the addy to the function?

Pink Lashes 11/30/2019

It's so annoying how pale I get in the winter months. Every woman of this burdened hue accepts we have two shades. That one concealer is trying but summer humidity.

Chock it up to stupidity. Lack of knowledge. Nah its not always college. Ensure you are always learning. Put up 20% so your pocket funds are not burning.

I told myself if one person shows up then this will have all been worth it. It was following a holiday. I wanted to quit and stop so many times. However, our oldest was also going through the process to further his football career. Forever the champion. I swallowed all the nonsense I was enduring and put my brave face on. I spoke words of encouragement even though I felt as if I was naked in front of white coats. I cleared my throat and squared my shoulders. I listened to my intro music. I just spoke from my heart. Now I know it's good to have bullet points. I was wiped out that day. The toll on my whole self was shaken. The feedback was positive. People had their souvenirs. For that day participants were shown genuine instruction from presenters who knew each topic intimately. The anointing was in the room. There were moments that day where I felt the same atmosphere that was planted in me in Denver, Colorado.

Dawn of the Dreadlocked Disciple

This is from the Book of Hebrews. You have two hands, correct?

These low vibes we reject like an application.

Witness her dedication to the preservation of a society who epitomize do over try. In front of many I opened my notebook.

Wasn't paying much attention to the importance of a snare.

Revelation 18:4. That wheel. 25 times four exponentially. Hypothetically, let me present to you the greatest mystery, faith. She is a wise big sister and she is more calm. Laptops producing atomic bombs. Let me give you this Los Angeles angelic melody that engages your pituitary gland. This is more than chakras although very important. Intuition is violet light surrounding your aura. Radiation from your Spirit envelopes me. In you, I believe. In you, I give my grief. In you, I rest. To You, we raise our hands in worship. We open our moves in honor of the ability to speak in tongues. Oya, Cuddy it has just begun. They were going to know our Big 3. Their ascension brought down the Trinity. Who yall thought our Father is?

Hard to roll a square, easier to stay in his will.

They call themselves #Harvoids. From his teaching they filled the void. Bridging the gap between whack and all that. Mac sauce on your meat. Created to be a help meet. Peace and companionship is her greeting. Just one meeting can change your life.

Bathsheba looked at Uriah like, "But I'm your wife". As a physician, it's always hard to see the dissolution. I've come to this notion:

Crabs in a bucket have claws and strong coverings. Moreover, they can grip. The promise is in the problem.

Journal Prompts:

1.   What is your current perspective of your tools?

1. Identify your top 3 talents

1. Write down what is presenting as a barrier to you utilizing your tools effectively?

1. How will you evaluate your current schema (thought pattern) emotions, and belief you have the capacity to allow God to fight your battles?

Glaciers Revelation 18:4 10/13/1992

Older than Phillis Wheatley, she did what others failed at; beautifully.

Skillfully, David positioned himself. He saw his opponent and smiled. Bro chuckled like this all you got. Between their eyes the diamond shattered upon contact.

The beauty that spewed from his forehead had the crowd in awe. Uncle from the Broad. It's a few that pull a wagon. Stroking the ears of a dragon. Purr sexier than a V8. Did you drink your V8?

Tomato, tomatoe. Catch a tiger by her big toe. You know all my points. I'll arch and point. Up in the air. In your face. Slide. Grind. Let me ride. Your neck. Your tongue on my back. Healing heart attacks with each stroke. My muffles you savor. The way you lick my throat. Open your pey. Pay me like I weigh.

Heavyweight cuz I'm a Disciple of Yahweh.

Colder than any berg. She from Jehovah Alcatraz. Swam that distance in 40 minutes flat. Nah, you can not handle this. Excuse me, Miss?

Disrespectful devil. Me and my walk with God so cold - you can not conceive my level. Unification of church and state already happened. Receive the word. I see your foot tappin.

Mats remind me of Kendrick Johnson. Threw my hoodie on and twerked. For justice Living legends came out of retirement.

Of course she's heaven sent. Wisdom is the other half of the same coin. West coast soil she was born. But officially, tray states coincidentally she birthed the covenant.

Journal Prompts:

1. Have you ever wondered what type of stone David used during his encounter with Goliath?

1. Which stance do you take as you review 1 Samuel 17:38-58. There are many passages in which you can tarry.

   1. Which scripture stood out to you in these passages of scripture?

Book of Philemon

Read the entire chapter for context to understand the following:

In Hebrew grammar the numerical value for our ability to create using our hands is 20. There are two meanings and sounds for the palms of our hands. For your consideration here is the meaning behind the power in your hands to destroy or create and restore.

Kahf/K/ pronounced as key

Khahf/Kh/pronounced as chutzpah. Chutzpah rhymes with "foot spa" or bravery that borders on rudeness is considered chutzpah. Your ability to experience the moments you envision resides in your hands. A cornerstone of achieving any goal is to write it down.

"As long ago as 1872, Francis Galton, the man behind eugenics and fingerprinting, reckoned that monarchs should live longer than the rest of us, since millions of people pray for the health of their King or Queen every day. His research showed just the opposite - no surprise, perhaps, given the indulgent diet and underlying stress of fending off threats to the throne that royals must endure. An oft-discussed 1988 study by cardiologist Randolph Byrd of San Francisco General Hospital took a more rigorous look at the same question and found that heart patients who were prayed for fared better than those who were not. But a larger study in 2005 by cardiologist Herbert Benson at Harvard University challenged that finding, reporting that complications occurred in 52% of heart bypass patients who received intercessory prayer and 51% of those who didn't - essentially a tie."

The author continues with, "But there is one thing on which both camps agree: when you're setting up your study, it matters a great deal whether subjects know they're being prayed for. Give them a hint as to whether they're in the prayer group or a control group, and the famed placebo effect can blow your data to bits."

(Can God and Medicine Work Together, Jeffrey Kluger, Time Magazine 2020 Special Edition, pages 74-77)

Journal Prompts:

1. What are your thoughts on this perspective?

1. Do you believe faith and medicine can work harmoniously in your life?

1. What spoke to you from this excerpt, and why?

Bathsheba

I really wasn't checking for nobody. I just savor the dawn. The still of the dawn. Each rising of the sun is another opportunity to sit a spell with you, Allah.

The melody of the birds silenced by your angel's dissension. Archangel Jerome clothed himself in human form. My eyes stopped burning. My mouth was moist. I licked my lips and tasted salty tears. Jerome said to me the words of Allen Wheelis, "A truly Christian position calls for the self denial, a renouncing or rejection of something or someone you love for power, requires one to give all he has to the poor, to love his enemy, to turn the other cheek. A measure of the instinctual force of the drive for power is given by the rarity with such an ethic that has in fact been practiced." (The Way We Were, Allen Wheelis, reprinted 2019)

She went to her prayer closet to commune with God. As she filled her tub with collected rainwater and rose petals. An arduous task that she enjoyed. It was the only time when the world was still. The dawn offered such a promise of opportunity. She knew if she remained steady in her faith, her husband's desire to pursue God would ignite.

He saw her from afar. He did not see the tears that ran down her cheeks. He was far off so he did not hear her sobs. He was far away and could not hear her moans. She recited the scripture, Romans 8:26, "Likewise the Spirit also helpeth our infirmities: for we know not what we should pray for as we ought: but the Spirit itself maketh intercession for us with groanings which cannot be uttered."

He watched her as she took her tarot card deck out. He watched how the sun reflected off of her honey complexion. Her hair was plaited. She unraveled her plaits and shook her head as if she was rebuking future toil. He watched as she let the petals fall from her fingers like dreams she wanted to purge her soul of. She fed her ori. She lifted her head to the East and thanked God for allowing her to see another dawn. Dusk turned into cold nights. She dipped her ring and pinky finger in the rose water. She poured goat's milk into the water as she hummed Hallelujah. She swirled the combination of roses, rainwater, her tears, and goat milk.

He was unable to move. He had danced in the Spirit many times. But this was different. He was unable to stop his gaze. She raised her eyes to the rays from the sun shining on her melanated skin. She sprinkled hibiscus flowers into the now creamy bath.

She crouched down and stretched. With the elegance of a private dancer she slid into the bath. Her red sea parted. He stared, enthralled. She was not a tall woman yet she stood heads and shoulders above the rest. She exhaled and smiled. Lovingly, she embraced the messages of heaven and earth. Her dreadlocks, now loose, unmoved by Oya's winds. She spread the deck. He etched her every move into his soul. He never wanted to forget a detail. Time stopped. He smiled. Her wings. Wow. The man that wrote the book of Psalms was speechless.

Scholars said the "real meaning of the Hebrew form of the name Bathsheba is not clear. The second part of the name appears in 1 Chronicles 3:5 as 'Shua'; there is a note to compare this to what was spoken in Genesis 28:2" (Morris, Prince et.al, Bathsheba. JewishEncyclopedia.com, Reprinted October 2020).

Typically Shua would do a large spread. This dawn she was weary of the incessant low vibes of the environment. The card she pulled was a male holding a tabernacle with his mouth. In His right hand sat His Son. His other Son sat on Gaia with the favor of Abba.

In Chronicles it says when David saw her, he "fell in love". Although she heard her husband before she saw Him; she exhaled and smiled. Shua sat the card down on her altar next to her anointed oil. She disrobed. As her flower patterned robe fell to the floor he gasped. Every dream, every vision, every accomplishment failed to hold a candle.

David felt Shua in a place he did not know existed. Light swallowed him up on the rooftop. David immediately started to develop his plan. Shua cupped her hands and allowed the water to pour over her face, taking with it her sorrows. Shua looked up and saw a figure far off. The water was still on her eyelids when she saw David. Their images of one another were distorted. Yet the feeling. Shua wanted to look away. Across rooftops. Across the noise. Across the pain. Across the past. God pierced them both. She felt the butterflies in her stomach. She finally broke the hold that seemed to clear her throat. Yes Lord were the only words that escaped her lips. She looked at her card on the table. The trinity reflected back at her.

Selah

David is an effective busybody. This time, David said to himself, "I'm Enoch and she is my wife." David employed all of his Machiavellian tactics. They all failed. It was not until he completely gave all of himself to God did he feel as if he deserved a woman of such pedigree.

The Bible says in 1 Kings 1: 11-31 that Bathsheba became the favored wife, and with the aid of Nathan, was able to obtain the succession-rights for her son Solomon. the key scripture in these passages for today is:

1 Kings 11:15 which states in the KJV "And Bathsheba went in unto the king into the chamber: and the king was very old; and Abishag the Shunammite ministered unto the king." Shua did not know this man had so many demons inside of him as she got closer. His face was that of a screaming flaming skull head. His desire to be set free from his legion was genuine. Tact has never been one of David's strongest suits. Upon further investigation of scrolls raided from our most recent excavation I found the writings of Luke.

Luke ruminated on where Bathsheba came from and why she was so alluring. Some say Bathsheba may mean "daughter of the oath"which is documented as being spelled as Bath - Shua".

Journal Prompts:

1. Do you have any hobbies that society could view as strange or weird?

1. How do you view your habits or rituals?

1. Are your practices getting you further or closer to your declared vision?

Ida Be Healed Magick

The black phlegm came out of her. She pulled the cankerworm from her intestines. As she exorcized the last demon, it spewed daggers. Her talons extended. Yet a drop of its venom fell on her lip. She fell to her knees and heaved.

Beeazlebub held onto the self proclaimed Champion. Silly serpent did not know we tread on low vibes. Let down the jet skis. Doing doughnuts around the yacht waiting for the rocket ship. Keep your mule. Have you seen her hips?

I need all the wisdom I can get. Google me Papi, stay in my pocket. I'm legit from the West Coast.

Central Los Angeles intelligence. Honoring our current leaders with elegance. They know I can get nasty. Teaching me there is a time and a place. Don't worry. Your face is my throne. Let me get you back in the castle. Went through all this hassle and you just wanted me to listen.

You got my undivided attention. The Coat of Arms may be a lil scarred but Joseph had a dream. What do you believe?

Blessings to Mrs. Naiomi. It's you and me. He is well taken care of by Maam. You just relax with Mama's Other Boys.

Bless the Lord, Oh my soul. And do not forget me. Some names are so sacred.

Therefore, faith is essential as she moves like the pillar she is. Wisdom heals and reveals herself to His promise. With your courage I am here. Obatala. All things he gives thought to he binds here on earth and in heaven. Whatever our Commander in Chief declares is loosed or bound in heaven and here on earth!!!!!!!!!!!

POW - POWER OF WORSHIP 6/12/2024

What's the fun in knowing forever? As long as you and I are together. Let faith be your tugboat. His yoke light. His way is my rite of passage. Classic like the pages of sacred scrolls. Your vision unfolds in a way that we boldly uphold.

On the shores of Kemet her heart longed. She always knew where she belonged. Archangels know the language of devils. New level, same God.

I shall not give credit where it is not deserved. Poe. You're disgusting bro. That's why God said, nevermore.

FREAKNICCC 1922

Shawty scooped up her Monk from the Corner and said I'm not going to Sojourner. Yall been holding me up since Rampart. Not even in the wooded district. Palm trees. Ocean air filled the breeze. On a telegram while sippin with Bell. Christ is the One to revere. I'm so sincere. Their eyes. Almond shaped slants got me snatched.

Waist train Tuesday. Its Ogun's day. In his suit. lower case g brought the lotus. He said. Yemaya. Athena. Gaia. Executive Coach K, on behalf of Yahweh I beseech thee.

I know what you did with Al-Baraqa. Om is what they're chanting. Open mouths that know pey sing hallelujah as they sway.

Red liquid poured as Hippocrates had described. My fangs made themselves known. My young passengers were getting restless. They stroked their phallices as blood poured from her cranium as DJ Khaos played. She was somewhere but not where she needed to be.

Anansi appeared and stated the purple lotus is believed to be mystic. I said do a calypso come with that thunder? I need a few thighs too. Give me some fries before you get through. I need all the sauces. Only mature cougars I'm tossin like Bingo coins. Wisdom got em speaking in tongues. In every language it's interpreted as:

We have found the one.

The eight petals of the purple lotus represent the Noble Eightfold Path, one of the most important teachings because the Purple lotus changes the hue of the White lotus.

The White lotus symbolizes Bodhi (being enlightened, or receiving the Holy Ghost). It also represents mental purity, spiritual perfection, and peace.

Please note that the Red lotus represents the HEART and symbolizes love and compassion.

The Blue lotus symbolizes a victory of the Spirit over that of wisdom, intelligence, and knowledge. In Buddhist artwork, blue lotuses are never fully open so as not to observe the center of the flower.

(Buddhism and the Lotus, www.earth.com[1], Reprinted 2019)

Journal Prompts:

What type of lotus flower are you?

What is the best type of soil (your heart) to encourage growth for your lotus?

What is preventing you from tending to your garden?

1.	http://www.earth.com

GENERAL NAT TURNER SOLAR ECLIPSE

If you say you love God, how can you hate your neighbor? Do you not both bleed red blood?

Lil red riding hood grew up to be the Butterfly reaper. Pulled up on her black steed.

Wisdom's words, at first they did not want to hear.

Like the Northridge quake she penetrated their cranium. Through their sacral passage she invaded. Some resisted. Most engaged. They knew the years after 2020 were too hard to repeat

.

Different melodies yet one song. One rhythm. One horn. The laughter of triumph. The courage of our forefathers and babes in God. We respect other ethnicities here. However, when you take that blessed oath; you are no longer a foreigner. This is God's country. Do not disrespect. Do not disrespect. Do not hinder. Do not hinder any that seek him. He has established His church here on the rock of the NEW-ish covenant. We are tried and true. No matter what we've been through.

We keep hope alive. Only the best survive. Yet our compassion allows for others to thrive. Too much attention has been given to foreign affairs. We are the goal. People around the globe seek our land to make their dreams come true. Yet, how do we still have poverty? Lack of education - people learn different ways.

Why are children being left behind if the goal is to push them through. Which is it?

The event in itself can be traumatic or an opportunity to learn. It is how you perceive and process the information that sets the next stage for your next decade.

Que Sara, Sarah

Mami good now. She is resting. Not before she made sure y'all knew that although our blood all runs red. Heed this simple truth.

Your job is to serve and protect. Do not forsake your commandment due to your unchecked ego. Do you need a rhyme? Pick up your Bible and go.

Anansi feels a tickle in the bottom of his foot. He likes that. He feels their energy. I recline my seat. Shout out to Elon for the self driving feature. I mean if all the creatures in hell look like her. I may be able to handle a couple of succubus. Or is it succubi?

Either way, can I get between your thighs? I don't usually do this. I've been all out of sorts since you came around. I'll be honest. I was waiting for you to fail. I wanted you to quit. Might as well thank the man up above for drones. Them birds eye views are glimpses of heaven.

Your inebriation is my invitation. It took me a minute but now I'm ready. She really does just kick it in cemeteries. Like who does that? Now here I am. In a fucking cemetery.

Found under carnal knowledge. She's an angel. Lord. If this is as close as I'm going to get to heaven here on earth, what will thou have me to do?

A mission. I understood the mission. But this. This wasn't expected. You're loyal to a fault. Some people care too much. Most don't care at all. She is light.

She complained to the doctor about her complexion. Douglass Huey spoke about the beast that grips Black people of my hue. We are the red headed step children of the Black community. The paper bag test really is a thing. The cold part is that I get the negatives of both sides. To add insult to injury they give me a name that most can not pronounce.

Too dark to pass because we still have our wide nostrils. Too light to be accepted because even though we lack the ability to camouflage in the dark; we've evolved to walk in the light.

She's always looking up at the sky. The sunlight glistened off those gorgeous thighs. Just the right combination of soft and hard. Strong enough to endure yet soft enough to still give from her empty cup.

My prayer Lord, if I may. Let her feel your love in the sun rays. Let the water soothe her soul and remind her she is firmly planted in You. Touch her heart Lord. Remind he that there is nothing too hard for You. Remind her that You count every tear and store them up. Remind her Lord. She needs to remember the good because the world needs her. Future generations need her.

Wisdom.

You speak the promise every time you fortify your problem. The lower case "t" also ends our title for Christ. When you breathe, you allow for your inner light to flow throughout your body. As your oxygen transforms within your cells; blood travels to your heart and mind, allowing for you to recognize that as a human we are limited. With Christ, we are limitless. However, the ability to be meek is the responsibility or Khaf to intergenerational healing and resilience.

Journal Prompts:

1. What is your understanding of your future literally being in the palm of your hands?

1. Have you ever felt your heart skip when you see the smile of a particular person?

1. Do you look at yourself and feel those same emotions when you look into your eyes, where I reside?

Thursday October 13, 1800 Operation Dixon

From the Quran in the Book of Al Fatihah which means 'the opening' in book 1:6 Lead us on the exact right path till we reach the goal, verse 7 continues with; The path of those whom You have bestowed Your blessings, those who have not incurred (Your) displeasure, and those who have not gone astray.

They really checking me again to get on this plane? I'm already waddling. It's hot. And just because of my name, I need additional screening? Of course she went with Barak. It cost her her sanity. She was just waiting for a windfall of money to come and give her some relief. People die in the wilderness. People die everyday with their goals being unfulfilled. People walk around everyday bleeding on other people. People walk around everyday with their swords drawn to cut foe or friend.

I'll be your companion. I stick closer than a friend. I've laid down my life for my brother many times. However, no more. Fair exchange is not robbery. You're not going to continue to silence the voices of the marginalized.

WARNING - THIS IS IN REGARDS TO SUICIDE and DOMESTIC VIOLENCE

She looks like life. The way she smiles. The way her countenance is so ferocious. She shifts the atmosphere. In hurting her, I hurt myself. So as my last fuck you, Ill put this rope around my neck. I'll make sure you find this tub full of blood and my lifeless body. You would not hear me in life. I will make sure you hear me in death.

They made a human rope to get the woman out of the ocean. She was good. She waded out, praying Poseidon would send a message that the pain is too great and she would not continue. It wasn't pride. It was a promise. Do not go gently into that good night.

From the fists of Dachau's dark prince she pried his golden hands off of her. She dared not look in the mirror at what her husband had done to remind her of staying in the bath for too long. His eggs were lukewarm. She did catch a glimpse of his recent handiwork. The bite marks on her body. The imprint of pawned rings on her face. The left side of Wisdom's face paralyzed. That's a cold trade off. *Insert Name* look like the dude from the cartoon. What was his name?

2 Faced Lawyer. Snooping around like Tom Sawyer. Bell's Palsy is what they call it. He was on my line blaming me for his hits. That's when he liked sex the most. Primitive heathen. How can a bruised and tattered body bring you pleasure? It's the demon blood in us all.

No point at being mad at any one character in any sacred texts. They were all jacked up. You are too. And It Is OK.

It is okay to not be okay. When you praise the daughter or son over the parent that contributed to the creation of the child your fruit fails to take root. I would not be able to speak to what I have not experienced. Life can sometimes appear chaotic. This is the time when you use your most valuable weapon, resting in peace.

Journal Prompts:

1. What is your default to most situations in your life?

1. How do you want your true loved ones to remember you now?

1. What are your 13 takeaways from this workshop?

COLLECTIVE CONSCIOUSNESS ILLUMINATION - if I give you this information now, what is the fun in waiting for the sequel?